Crabby Gabby

 **Crabtree Publishing Company**
www.crabtreebooks.com

PMB16A, 350 Fifth Avenue
Suite 3308,
New York, NY

616 Welland Avenue
St. Catharines, ON
L2M 5V6

Published by Crabtree Publishing in 2008

First published in 2006 by
Franklin Watts
(A division of Hachette Children's Books)
338 Euston Road
London   NW1 3BH

Cataloging-in-Publication data is available at the Library of Congress.

ISBN 978-0-7787-3852-7 (rlb)
ISBN 978-0-7787-3883-1 (pbk)

Series Editor: Jackie Hamley
Series Advisor: Dr Hilary Minns
Series Designer: Peter Scoulding

Printed in the U.S.A.

Crabby Gabby

by Sue Graves

Illustrated by Desideria Guicciardini

Crabtree Publishing Company

www.crabtreebooks.com

Sue Graves

"Do you ever get crabby like Gabby? It's not a very nice feeling, is it? Luckily, Gabby's much better behaved now and never gets crabby at all!"

Desideria Guicciardini

"I was born in a castle in Florence in Italy. I like drawing angry ladies. I never eat puddings and I'm almost always in a good mood."

Gabby was always grumpy.

Everyone called her Crabby Gabby.

7

Mom asked her to dry the dishes.

Gabby got crabby.

Dad asked her
to clean her room.

Gabby got crabby.

Grandma asked her to feed the dog.

Gabby got very crabby!

Then her family had
a good idea.

When Gabby asked her family to play a game with her ...

... they all got crabby!

Gabby was sorry.

Now Gabby's not crabby anymore!

Notes for adults

TADPOLES are structured to provide support for early readers. The stories may also be used by adults for sharing with young children.

Starting to read alone can be daunting. **TADPOLES** help by providing visual support and repeating high frequency words and phrases. These books will both develop confidence and encourage reading and rereading for pleasure.

If you are reading this book with a child, here are a few suggestions:

1. Make reading fun! Choose a time to read when you and the child are relaxed and have time to share the story.
2. Talk about the story before you start reading. Look at the cover and the blurb. What might the story be about? Why might the child like it?
3. Encourage the child to reread the story, and to retell the story in their own words, using the illustrations to remind them what has happened.
4. Discuss the story and see if the child can relate it to their own experiences, or perhaps compare it to another story they know.
5. Give praise! Children learn best in a positive environment.

If you enjoyed this book, why not try another TADPOLES story?

At the End of the Garden
9780778738503 RLB
9780778738817 PB

Bad Luck, Lucy!
9780778738510 RLB
9780778738824 PB

Ben and the Big Balloon
9780778738602 RLB
9780778738916 PB

Crabby Gabby
9780778738527 RLB
9780778738831 PB

Five Teddy Bears
9780778738534 RLB
9780778738848 PB

I'm Taller Than You!
9780778738541 RLB
9780778738855 PB

Leo's New Pet
9780778738558 RLB
9780778738862 PB

Little Troll
9780778738565 RLB
9780778738879 PB

Mop Top
9780778738572 RLB
9780778738886 PB

My Auntie Susan
9780778738589 RLB
9780778738893 PB

My Big, New Bed
9780778738596 RLB
9780778738909 PB

Pirate Pete
9780778738619 RLB
9780778738923 PB

Runny Honey
9780778738626 RLB
9780778738930 PB

Sammy's Secret
9780778738633 RLB
9780778738947 PB

Sam's Sunflower
9780778738640 RLB
9780778738954 PB